SpongeBob SquarePants

"Just Say Cheese!"

illustrated by Harry Moore

Ready-to-Read

Simon Spotlight/Nickelodeon

New York   London   Toronto   Sydney

Stephen Hillenburg

Based on the TV series *SpongeBob SquarePants*® created by Stephen Hillenburg as seen on Nickelodeon®

SIMON SPOTLIGHT
An imprint of Simon & Schuster Children's Publishing Division
1230 Avenue of the Americas, New York, New York 10020
Manufactured in the United States of America
6 8 10 9 7 5
Library of Congress Cataloging-in-Publication Data
Willson, Sarah.
Just say please! / by Sarah Willson ; illustrated by Harry Moore. – 1st ed.
p. cm. – (Ready-to-read)
"Based on the TV series SpongeBob SquarePants created by Stephen Hillenburg as seen on Nickelodeon."
ISBN-13: 978-1-4169-4129-3
ISBN-10: 1-4169-4129-0
I. Moore, Harry. II. SpongeBob SquarePants (Television program) III. Title.
PZ7.W6845Jr 2007
2006031896

"What's wrong, Pearl?"
asked SpongeBob.
"Tomorrow is Parents' Day at school,"
sobbed Pearl, "and my dad
wants to come!"

"But what is wrong with Mr. Krabs coming?" asked SpongeBob.

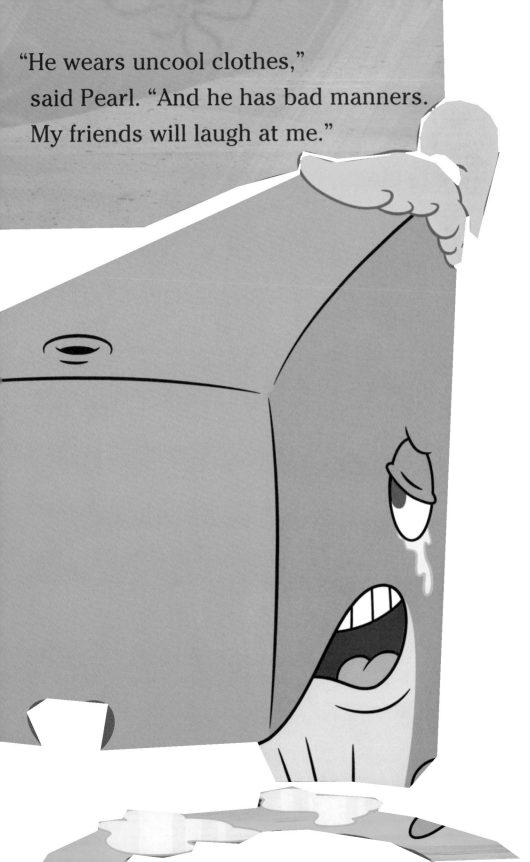

"He wears uncool clothes,"
said Pearl. "And he has bad manners.
My friends will laugh at me."

Just then Mr. Krabs called out,
"SpongeBob, get me some grub!"
"Yes, sir! Right away, sir!"
said SpongeBob.

SpongeBob went to the kitchen and
whipped up a Krabby Patty.
"Here you go, sir,"
said SpongeBob.
"Umph," said Mr. Krabs. He did not say
"thank you."

"You are right about Mr. Krabs,"
   Squidward said to Pearl.
"He does have bad manners.
   And his clothes are worn out.
   Maybe you need to go
   to a new school."

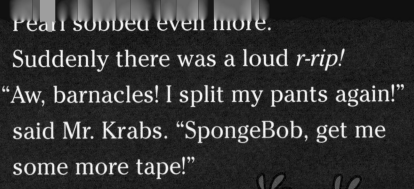

Pearl sobbed even more.
Suddenly there was a loud *r-rip!*
"Aw, barnacles! I split my pants again!"
said Mr. Krabs. "SpongeBob, get me
some more tape!"

"Uh, Pearl, I will help you,"
whispered SpongeBob.
"Squidward and I will give him
a makeover."

"We will?" said Squidward.

"Oh, SpongeBob!" said Pearl.

"That would be just swell."

A short while later SpongeBob burst
into the office.

"Mr. Krabs! Guess what? The queen
is coming to the Krusty Krab!"

"Which queen?" asked Mr. Krabs.

12

"Oh, uh, just a queen," replied
SpongeBob. "But don't worry.
I will help you study this
manners book. You will know
just what to do."

They read the book.

Mr. Krabs learned to say "please."

He learned to say "thank you."

He learned how to greet someone politely.

"Good manners are hard work!"
grumbled Mr. Krabs.

The next day SpongeBob and
Squidward took Mr. Krabs
to the mall.
They helped him choose
a new outfit.

"Why do I need a new outfit?"
asked Mr. Krabs.
"Because you are going to see
the queen," SpongeBob replied.
"Oh, okay," said Mr. Krabs.

"You really stand out,
    Mr. Krabs," said Squidward.
"Why, thank you!" said Mr. Krabs.

"Hey, maybe you can wear this
to Parents' Day tomorrow too!"
SpongeBob said.

19

At lunchtime the queen arrived.
Mr. Krabs was so nervous
he did not notice that
the queen was really Squidward
all dressed up!

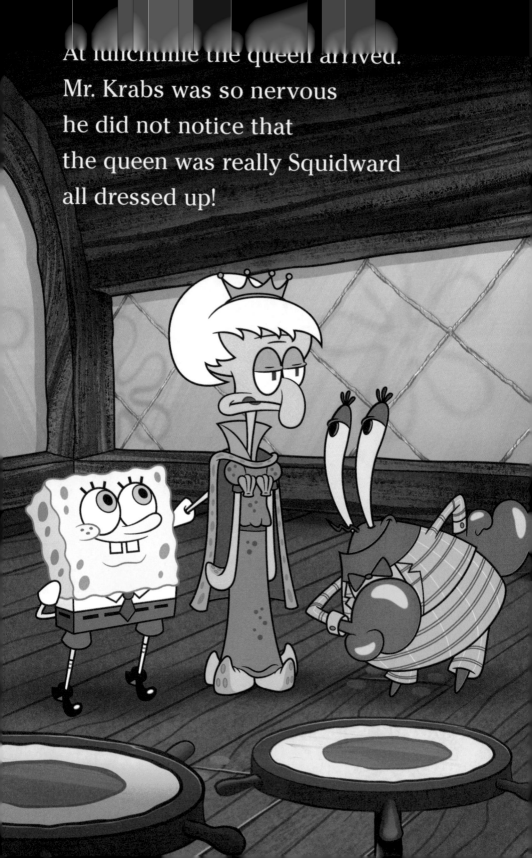

He greeted the "queen"
with a bow.
He held out her chair for her.
He said "please" and "thank you."
And he did not even charge her
for refills on water!

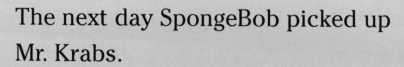

The next day SpongeBob picked up
Mr. Krabs.

"Do I look okay?" asked Mr. Krabs.

"You sure do!" said SpongeBob.

"Thank you, SpongeBob. I want Pearl
to be proud of me," said Mr. Krabs.
"I am sure she will be," said SpongeBob.

"Pearl, is that your dad
    in that funny outfit?"
    asked Pearl's friend Jen.
    Pearl gasped. "No! I mean, it *can't* be!"
"Hello, Pearl!" said Mr. Krabs.
"Is this a friend of yours?"

He bowed low and then said,
"How do you do?"
Jen giggled.

Pearl watched her father greet
her friends. He bowed.

He said "please" and "thank you."
He even refilled her teacher's water glass!

Mr. Krabs tugged at SpongeBob's arm. "Good manners are hard work," he whispered. "And these new clothes feel tight. But I will do anything for Pearl."

ting weird!
Please change him back!"
SpongeBob was surprised,
but he said, "Okay, Pearl."

29

A while later Mr. Krabs came back,
wearing his old clothes.
"Oh, Daddy!" said Pearl.
"You look coral!"

Mr. Krabs beamed. "Lead me to the grub!" he said.

"Thanks for trying, SpongeBob," said Pearl. "You are a true friend. But you really should think about getting a new tie."